Text copyright © 2008 Amber Stewart
Illustrations copyright © 2008 Layn Marlow
First published in Great Britain in 2008 by Oxford University Press

Library of Congress Cataloging-in-Publication Data is available.

ISBN-13: 978-0-545-12991-6
ISBN-10: 0-545-12991-5

10 9 8 7 6 5 4 3 2 1   09 10 11 12 13

Printed in China
Reinforced Binding for Library Use
First Scholastic edition, April 2009

Amber Stewart & Layn Marlow

Bedtime for Button

ORCHARD BOOKS • NEW YORK
An Imprint of Scholastic Inc.

Button was ready for bed.

"My little bear cub must be tired," said Mommy,
"after such a busy day."

"Sweet dreams," said Daddy.

Button thought about his day
and wondered what his
dreams might bring.

He remembered the
early morning sunshine . . .

climbing with his
big sisters . . .

playing by their
favorite pool . . .

and finding
interesting insects.

That's when Button first saw the big, scary tree-bear.

Button had forgotten about the
scary tree-bear until that very moment.
Suppose it came into his dreams tonight?

He couldn't take the risk.

"Mommy! Daddy!" he called.

Button told them about the scary tree-bear.

Daddy said, "Should I give you
something nice to think about
before you go to sleep?
Nice thoughts always keep
the bad ones away."

"Yes please." Button nodded,
feeling much braver about
the scary tree-bear.

"Well," wondered Daddy, "should I tell you about
a day when there were no scary things?
A day so happy that if you think of it tonight,
only sweet dreams will come."

"What day was that, Daddy?" asked Button,
tickling Daddy's fur as he wriggled his toes.
Daddy kissed the top of his nose and said,
"The day you were born . . ."

"It was one of those days that started foggy, but I knew a hot and sunny day was just around the corner."

"A little like today?" asked Button.
"When I woke up, I couldn't even
see over the berry bush!"

"Yes, just like today." Daddy smiled. "And on the day you were born,
I gathered the juiciest berries and stickiest honey."

"A little like today?" asked Button,
as he remembered lying in
the warm sun, eating his sweet
breakfast berries.

"Yes," said Daddy, "but even more delicious."

"On the day you were born,"
Daddy continued, holding Button's paw, "your big sisters
were so happy, they found special presents for you. . . ."

"Like my lucky pinecone," said Button,
"and my little log boat! And did they want
to play with me, too?"

"Oh yes!" laughed Daddy. "They wanted to play
with you right then and there, but Mommy
said you needed to grow a little first . . ."

"And now I've grown!" said Button.
"We played so much today,
we had to jump in
Two Rivers Pool to cool down."

"When evening came," said Daddy,
"I remember I took you in my arms to watch your
first-ever sunset and sing you a lullaby."

"Just like every evening." Button yawned.
He loved watching the sun go down with Daddy
and singing songs that made them laugh.

"And on your very first night," said Daddy quietly,
"you were so tired you fell fast asleep. Mommy
and I watched you, and no bad dreams
came to disturb our little one."

"Just like tonight?" said sleepy Button.

"Yes," whispered Daddy.

And Daddy was right . . .

only sweet dreams came.